# STAR WARS™

## TALES OF THE FORCE

by Christopher Nicholas

illustrated by Ron Cohee, Chris Kennett, Patrick Spaziante,
Heather Martinez, Ethen Beavers, Tyler Keshner, and Seung Kim

 A GOLDEN BOOK • NEW YORK

© & ™ 2017 LUCASFILM LTD. All rights reserved. Published in the United States by Golden Books, an imprint of Random House Children's Books, a division of Penguin Random House LLC, 1745 Broadway, New York, NY 10019, and in Canada by Penguin Random House of Canada Limited, Toronto, in conjunction with Disney Enterprises, Inc. Golden Books, A Golden Book, A Big Golden Book, the G colophon, and the distinctive gold spine are registered trademarks of Penguin Random House LLC.
ISBN 978-1-5247-7090-7
randomhousekids.com
Printed in the United States of America
10 9 8 7 6 5 4 3 2 1

**A long time ago in a galaxy far, far away . . .**
there were brave heroes and sinister villains
fighting an epic battle between good and evil.
Some were noble protectors of peace.

Others were power-hungry brutes who spread hatred and fear.

But they all relied on the power of the Force—an energy field created by all living things.

Gather your courage and prepare to meet these beings of the dark and the light from the *Star Wars* universe!

Jedi Knights were guardians who fought for peace and justice. They came from many different planets and stood together to protect the galaxy.

The Jedi Order was guided by the Jedi Council, which was made up of wise and powerful Jedi Masters.

A Jedi's power came from the Force—
an energy field created by all living things
that bound the galaxy together.

A Jedi could use the Force to move and
levitate objects. While learning the ways of
the Jedi, rebel hero Luke Skywalker levitated
rocks and crates—and even his astromech
droid, R2-D2!

The Jedi Master Yoda was so powerful
that he was able to use the Force to lift
a huge X-wing starfighter out of a swamp!

Jedi could use the power of the Force to perform amazing physical feats. They could run extremely fast and jump very high or across long distances.

Feeling the Force flow through him, Luke Skywalker leapt and flipped throughout the swamp on planet Dagobah.

The Force was particularly strong in Jedi Master Mace Windu. He was a powerful warrior respected by his allies— and feared by his enemies.

Even a fierce bounty hunter like Jango Fett was no match for Master Windu!

The Force was so powerful that Jedi could even use it to control the weak-minded! Obi-Wan Kenobi used a Jedi mind trick to escape Imperial stormtroopers at the Mos Eisley spaceport.

Years later, Luke Skywalker used the Force to enter the palace of crime lord Jabba the Hutt. The Jedi Knight took control of the mind of Jabba's attendant Bib Fortuna, who led him straight to the gigantic gangster!

The Resistance hero Rey used the Force to make a
First Order stormtrooper release her from her cell.

Jedi could be recognized by the hooded cloaks they wore. Jedi Master Mace Windu and Jedi Knight Qui-Gon Jinn wore brown robes as they protected the planets in the Galactic Republic.

Some Jedi were very tall, while others were quite small.
But Jedi should never be judged by their size. The Jedi
Masters Yoda, Yaddle, and Even Piell were among the
smallest and most powerful Jedi who ever lived!

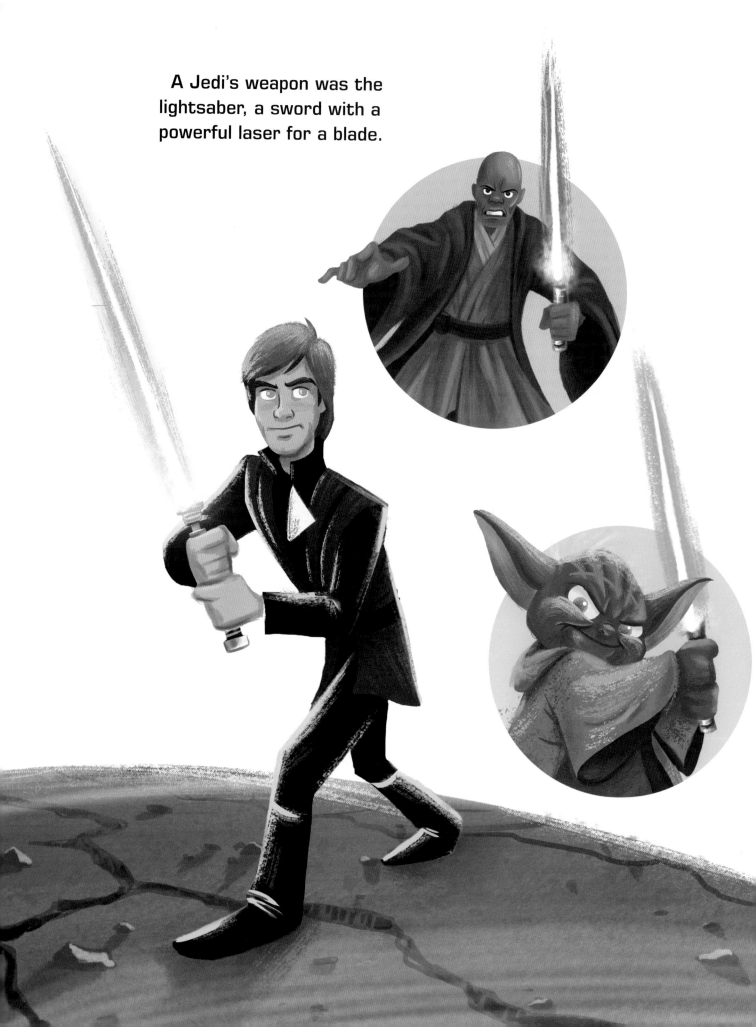

A Jedi's weapon was the lightsaber, a sword with a powerful laser for a blade.

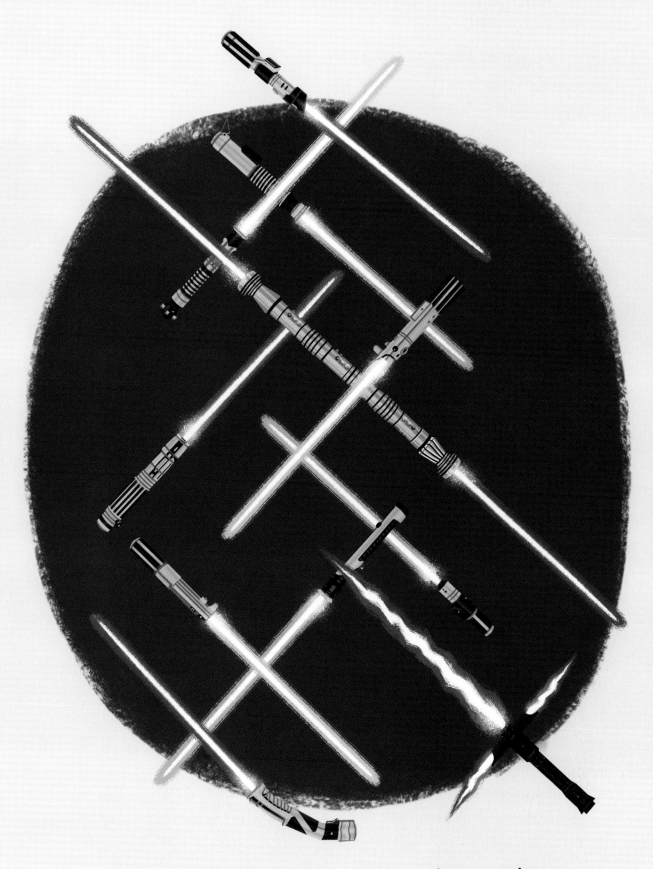

Lightsabers could be many different shapes, colors, and sizes. They received their power from crystals that were in tune with the Force.

A Jedi could use
a lightsaber to duel
with enemies . . .

deflect a laser
blast . . .

or cut through anything!

Jedi Knights Obi-Wan Kenobi and Qui-Gon Jinn used their lightsabers to protect the people of Naboo from the Trade Federation and their droid army!

Some Jedi were very young. A young Jedi in training was called a Padawan. Anakin Skywalker was only nine years old when he began to learn the ways of the Force from Jedi Knight Obi-Wan Kenobi.

Some Jedi were very old. Jedi Master Yoda was more than 800 years old when he instructed Padawans before the Clone Wars!

At the end of their lives, all Jedi became one with the Force. Some continued to communicate with the living as Force Spirits!

Jedi Master Obi-Wan Kenobi sacrificed himself to the Imperial commander Darth Vader . . .

. . . and he continued to guide Luke Skywalker
in the ways of the Force for years to come.

Throughout their lives, Jedi must always be brave. While rescuing rebel hero Han Solo, Jedi Knight Luke Skywalker faced the colossal crime lord Jabba the Hutt . . .

. . . and his monstrous pet rancor!

A Jedi should be calm and at peace.
Fighting was the last resort for the Jedi.

Jedi Knight Qui-Gon Jinn always took time to meditate—even
while defending Queen Amidala from the savage Darth Maul!

Hate and fear could lead a Jedi down the path toward the dark side of the Force! Jedi Knight Anakin Skywalker gave in to his hate when he attacked the sand people who captured his mother. This was his first step to becoming . . . a Sith!

The Sith were the enemy of the Jedi. They were evil warriors who used the Force to spread fear. The Jedi were in a constant battle with the Sith to restore balance to the Force.

There could be only two Sith Lords at a time—a master and an apprentice. During his reign of terror, the Sith Lord Emperor Palpatine had several apprentices.

Palpatine's first apprentice was Darth Maul, a savage warrior with a double-bladed crimson lightsaber. Maul followed his evil master's bidding without question.

When Darth Maul was defeated by Jedi Knight Obi-Wan Kenobi, he was replaced by a Jedi Knight named Count Dooku. As Palpatine's new apprentice, Dooku took the Sith name Darth Tyranus!

But the Emperor's greatest apprentice of all was the Jedi Knight Anakin Skywalker— who came to be known as Darth Vader!

After a lightsaber battle with the Jedi Master Obi-Wan Kenobi, Darth Vader was badly injured. The Emperor gave him a special suit that helped to keep him alive—and made him look terrifying!

As a Sith apprentice to Emperor Palpatine, Darth Vader oversaw the creation of two gigantic battlestations—the Death Stars! At the Emperor's command, Vader destroyed almost all the Jedi in the galaxy.

The Emperor even ordered Vader to
destroy his own son, Luke Skywalker.

Just as a Jedi could become a Sith, sometimes a Sith could escape the clutches of the dark side of the Force.

When the Emperor attacked his son, Darth Vader felt the good inside him return. He sacrificed his own life to defeat Palpatine—and save Luke!

Darth Vader became Anakin Skywalker once again.
He rejoined his old teachers Yoda and Obi-Wan Kenobi
in the light side of the Force.

Some Force users were neither Jedi nor Sith. Kylo Ren was a dark side warrior who served the evil First Order. Whether wielding his red lightsaber or at the controls of his TIE silencer, Kylo was determined to wipe out the Resistance.

Before becoming Kylo Ren, the villain was a Jedi trainee named Ben Solo—son of rebel leaders Princess Leia and Han Solo. Ben learned the ways of the Force from his uncle, Luke Skywalker. But Ben was drawn away from the light side of the Force . . .

. . . by Snoke, the Supreme Leader of the First Order! Snoke was a master of evil and commanded his armies from a secret location, protected by his crimson-armored elite guard.

Sometimes the Force could be very strong
in someone without them even knowing.

A young desert scavenger
named Rey was drawn into
the battle between the dark
and the light. She rescued
a droid named BB-8 . . .

ran into a runaway
stormtrooper
named Finn . . .

. . . met Resistance heroes
Han Solo and Chewbacca . . .

and became a hero for the
Resistance herself!

Sometimes a place could be strong with the Force. The planet Ahch-To was the home of an ancient Jedi temple that had been watched over by alien caretakers for ages.

After Kylo Ren destroyed all of his students, Jedi Master Luke Skywalker fled to Ahch-To to find peace in the Force.

Rey and Chewbacca flew off on a special mission to Ahch-To to find the missing Jedi Master. The Resistance needed Luke's help in their battle against the First Order.

Rey hoped to be trained in the ways of the Force and become a Jedi one day.

As long as there are Sith spreading hatred and fear, there will be Jedi fighting to bring balance to the Force.

And as long as there is good and evil in the galaxy, there will always be a battle between the dark and the light.